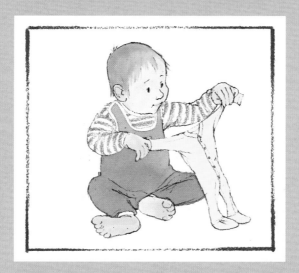

Other Lothrop, Lee & Shepard Books
by Jan Ormerod
Sunshine, Moonlight, Rhymes Around the Day,
101 Things to Do with a Baby, The Story of Chicken Licken

First U.S. Edition
1 2 3 4 5 6 7 8 9 10

Library of Congress Cataloging in Publication Data
Ormerod, Jan.   Mom's home!
Summary: When Mom comes back from shopping, a baby enjoys going
through her shopping basket.
[1. Mother and child—Fiction.   2. Babies—Fiction]   I. Title.
PZ7.0634Mn   1987   [E]   87-2712
ISBN 0-688-07274-7

Mom's Home
Jan Ormerod

LOTHROP, LEE & SHEPARD BOOKS
NEW YORK

Mom's home.

What's in her basket?

Things for a baby.

And what else?

Dig deep.

Wipe Mom's nose.

Have a banana…

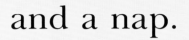

and a nap.

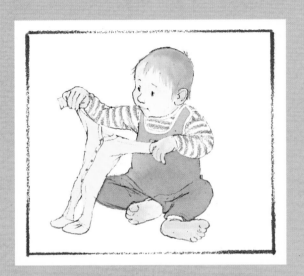